Designed by Providence

A Novella by:
Austin Mardon

Edited by:
Austin A. Mardon, Ernest G. Mardon,
& Claire MacMaster

Golden Meteorite Press

A Golden Meteorite Press Book.

Edited by Austin A. Mardon, Ernest G. Mardon & Claire MacMaster
Cover design and Typeset by Bianca Ho

Published by Golden Meteorite Press.
126 Kingsway Garden ,Post Office Box 34181
Edmonton, Alberta, CANADA, T5G 3G4
Telephone: 1-(780)-378-0063
Email: aamardon@yahoo.ca
Web site: www.austinmardon.org

Library and Archives Canada Cataloguing in Publication

Mardon, Austin, b. 1892
     Designed by providence : a novella / by Austin Mardon ; edited by
Austin A. Mardon, Ernest G. Mardon, & Claire MacMaster.

ISBN 978-1-897472-90-3

     I. Mardon, Austin A. (Austin Albert) II. Mardon, Ernest G., 1928-
III. MacMaster, Claire IV. Title.

PS8576.A6462D45 2012   C813'.54   C2012-905320-1

Dedicated to Mimi Mardon

Editor's Note

This manuscript has only just come into my posses-
sion, after being discovered among family papers in a remote
Highland Glen. My research reveals that the author, the late
professor Austin Mardon, was born in 1892 in Gloucestershire, England and was educated at Clifton College. He joined
the 5th Battalion "Mardon's Own" of the Gloucestershire Regiment at the outbreak of WWI and saw active service in German
East Africa with the Legion of Frontiersmen. He was seriously
wounded in action. Later in the war, he served with the Win-
nipeg Rifles in Europe. The records of Cambridge University
show he graduated in history with a Master of Arts degree in
1925. Professor Mardon lectured first at Cornell University
and later at Rice University in Houston, Texas. After he retired, he and his family moved to a remote glen, Ross-shire,
Scotland. It is believed he died in the early 1960s.

Designed by Providence

Contents

Part One

So little is worth recording if one were to spread one's observation in uniform strength over equal divisions of time. The surface of language has the monotony of belting, semi-rigid as it rotates between two otherwise unconnected pieces of machinery. And then something happens, and one sees more than the surface, hears more than a word ground out from a dictionary. Time and a machine have brought one to a series of moments that can be read, marked, learned and inwardly digested.

In an echo from church-going childhood, one is reminded to make his testimony. The observer sets down his vision, and if he is poor, ambitious or simply precocious, he imparts his knowledge to the world. The author reveals the time in which he lives.

Attached to his vision there are the dictionary words, the only tools with which he has to convey – like a belting power – his meaning. He is recompensed only if published. Words must be treated with care, for they report the daily unimportant surface, but keep their buried way about them.

I sent my baggage through to London, climbed the steep slopes within the Central Station, Glasgow. As we rumbled along, I read a collection of correspondences from an acquaintance who was stationed in Italy. These letters by this point were many years old, as I had no desire to prioritize my response.

He worked as a clerk in a war office, determining which rations would go where, and I suppose in a wider sense the fate of the many who rely on his organizational skills. Most of his letters took on the drawl tone of an administrator. He would offer reports on the enormous quantity of apples consumed by the regiment, and complaints about the shortage of meat.

"That damn fruit couldn't hope to feed a cat...let alone an army, all water it is." I could hear his voice in the timbre of his words and the thin signature at the bottom of the page, C. Vanier. I suppose it was a function of my mind, keen to fill in the emptiness in Vanier's sentences, but I found myself thinking of cattle roaming the streets of a coastal Italian town. They seemed too innocent, now knowing what their purpose was. I was wondering about the moral consequences of my thinking this way. Was it not to promote at least a lingering sense of dignity when a man's stomach is broken into with a bayonet? Cattle are slaughtered neatly, with a semblance of the need for hygiene that so frequently marks our age. What seemed more ridiculous to me I was not sure, the slaughtering of a beast in a brutal manner or to kill it neatly and carve with carefully sterilized knives. The letters could not afford to take on those tinges of humanity, which cause us to break free from our calculated rage and flee to the ruined streets, muttering a collective "why?"

He did mention briefly a "Principessa", someone he spoke of with a great deal of indifference, as if it were a title similar to "sergeant" or "lieutenant" in the military field. However, there was some indication in his letter that there were smiles exchanged between the two, perhaps undeserved on his part. I thought about this for a while and considered that if a smile could noteworthy in Vanier's account, then it must have been an exceptional smile. Vanier was lead to believe that she wore black dresses in honor of her late husband, an Englishman. She had a child who lived down the street from the office, strange as most families with children had long since moved into the country to ensure the safety of their offspring. Life to Vanier was a series of disorganized events that he was determined to pigeonhole into a manageable system, and thus he recounted the exact sightings of this little girl in exhausting detail. She walked with a limp and hung off the dress of her mother as to ensure her balance.

"Water sir?" the young attendant asked. I declined, citing a desire to sleep. The attendant nodded without a sense of acknowledgment. I felt silly for giving an excuse for my declining her offer. I settled back in my seat and continued reading letters, in the back of my mind I wished for more coffee and not water. I was filled with an unprecedented amount of regret.

Our friendship was maintained in the beginning by my goodwill. We attended the same school together and in my naïve concern for his social health I proposed that we ought maintain our relationship in the interests of mutual professional opportunities. I suppose it was in the interests also of preserving part of my college experience. Time was like the train heaving around me, staggering on into the future, taking brief, eventful stops that are retained in memory.

I could see the emotion and affection coloring the fringes of his prose when the Principessa turned up in the pages, he stopped quantifying and began to describe her features, which were light and seemed to transcend the limitations set by numbers and measurements. My answer to his letters was brief, apologizing for my tardy response. I recounted the events of the last few days, the things that I ate and their quality. It seemed to be the little things that make up the bulk of our lives, so I recounted them for posterity. The weather was a topic I tended to ignore, for it was as impersonal as the city you lived in.

I found myself in a sort of despair that was made pleasant by my feeling of self-righteousness in the face of my acquaintance's shortcomings. In this late stage before sleep it was easy for to forget myself and allow small moral indulgences.

I slept through the afternoon and evening as the train carried me through sunrise and sunset to the Black Country. I had in the course of my reading been much attracted by the account my Defoe had given of the England of his day – on the eve of change. Take this picture of his walk into Halifax:

> After we had passed the second hill, and come down into the valley again, and so still the nearer we came to Halifax we found the houses thicker, and the villages greater in every bottom; and not only so but the sides of the hills which were very steep every way, were spread with houses; for the land being divided into small enclosures, from two Acres to six or seven each, seldom more; every three or four pieces of land had a house belonging to them.

> In short, after we had mounted the Chird Hill, we found the country on continued village, tho' every way mountainous, hardly a house standing out of a speaking-distance from another as the day cleared up, we could see at every house a tenter, and on almost every tenter a piece of cloth, kersie or shalloon, which are the three articles of this country's labour.

> In the course of our road among the Houses, we found at every one of them a little rill of butter of running water, and at every considerable house was a manufactory, which not being able to be carried on without water, these little streams were so parted and guided by gut-

ters of pipes, that not one of the houses wanted its necessary appendage of a rivulet.

Again, as the dying-houses, scouring-shops, and places where they use this water, emit it ting'd with the drugs of the dying-vat, and with the oil, the soap, the tallow, and the other ingredients used by the clothiers in dressing and scouring etc. The land through which it passes, which otherwise would be exceedingly barren are enrich'd by it to a degree beyond imagination.

Then, as every clothier must necessarily keep on horse, at least, to fetch him his wool and his provisions from the market, to carry his yarn to the spinners, his manufacture to the fulling-mill, and when finished to the market to be sold, and the like, so every one generally keeps a cow or two for his family. By this means the small pieces of enclosed land about each house are occupied and by being thus fed, are still further improved from the dung of the cattle. As for corn, they scarce sow enough to feed their cocks and hens.

The place then seems to have been designed by providence for the very purposes to which it is now allotted, for carrying on a manufacture, which can nowhere be so easily supplied with the conveniences necessary for it. Nor is the industry of the people wanting to second these advantages.

Tho' we met few people without doors, yet within we saw the houses full of lusty fellows, some at the dye-vat, some at the loom, others dressing the cloths: the women and children carding or spinning; all employed from the youngest to the oldest, scarce anything above four years old, but its hands were sufficient for its own support.

Not a beggar to be seen, not an idle person, except here and there in an alms-house, built for those that are ancient and past working. The people in general live long: they enjoy a good air, and under such circumstances hard labour is naturally attended with the blessing of health, if not riches.

And then there was a rapid slowing of the express; the contents of the racks swayed and jolted; there was a noisy stop and escape of steam. In my drowsy state, which I hope I have not conveyed in the thoughts that had previously occupied us; I wondered for a moment whether we had not been moving perpendicularly rather than horizontally and had arrived at the bottom of a pit one hundred and seventy miles from Glasgow. How fortunate that our earlier scientists had presumably lacked something in their diet that had kept their movements one way rather than the other. Perhaps too much orange juice had led to the atomic bomb.

In the dusk which now danced along the fringes of this summer's day I saw, on lowering the window and looking out, that our portion of the train had drawn up opposite a station sign. We were at the platform end of the junction from which shuttled an infrequent train to Lambton. Rumour was reaching my ears, it told of a derailment further on, and the unlikelihood of the wheels under our feet continuing. An authoritative voice followed the whispers of concern. Those around me froze into a listening posture. Passengers were to be moving along in half an hour and a relay train was due to take us on. After the voice crackled out, the passengers blurred the outline of the news with conjecture. There was a train coming from the south and the two trains would exchange passengers. Meanwhile other trains would be re-routed. It had been a train of goods, only a few minutes ahead of us that had left a heap of material piled up across the permanent route. A local who had left mere minutes ahead had not been involved. Certainty quickly emerged from the nebulae of inference.

How many broken journeys were to be involved, I was never to know, for I had the curiosity to ask of someone outside how far it was to Lambton.

"No train 'til the morning." I was answered, "But if you move quickly and haven't any heavy luggage, there's a car outside the entrance ready to leave that'll take you there."

Two requirements asked of me, both of which I could satisfy, speed and no equipment. There was the intangible, pervasive connection of destiny binding us together, if one was not too slow and another not too quick. Flushed with my decision, I jumped from the train and without breaking into a quicker stride, to which my companions are accustomed, I found myself in the beam of a still stationary car.

"Are you for hire?" I asked, for that had not been a point of mention. "I was told you are going to Lambton."

"Yes, the fare will be ten shillings and I'll be glad of your company," was the answer.

I stepped in, computing the distance to be about fifteen miles.

"You nearly missed me," the driver at my side continued, as we started to move. "Take some time to make up your mind? Not so quick as you'll find the people around here. Our minds move fast – near enough to Lancashire – Lancashire man myself. There was an opening fifteen years ago for a mechanic. Gratuity after the war enabled me to start a garage. We'll pass it on the way. 'Spitfire.' They name a guarantee of the size of the gratuity I've put into the shed. 'Spitfire Shed' wouldn't sound so good. Like to hear the news?"

I imagined that some button would be pulled or pressed but the driver kept his hands on the wheel. And it may not be without interest to know what had been recorded, worthy of a mechanic's memory, on Thursday the 19th of July 1951. A file of the *Manchester Guardian* opened at that date might verify the references.

"Thank you very much," I said, when he seemed disposed to let the dust of the present settle on the dust of the past. He recounted the events of the previous day with animated self-involvement. "Yesterday must have been a very interesting day and I don't think any the worse of Lancashire for remembering it for twenty-four hours," I said with undeserved enthusiasm.

"Twenty-four hours?" he exclaimed. "Why, you'd be surprised. Where do you want to be dropped?"

"Well, where would you recommend?"

"'The Trout Inn' you'd have pretty well to yourself, and I would be doing a favour to Mrs. Cotton by putting you up there,"

"There I'll go then, and I'll thank you on her behalf as well as my own for settling the matter. Are you out often as late as this?"

"Not once in a month, the 'twenty-four hours service' isn't worth the paint it's painted with. No one would impose to that extent. But once in a while someone is stuck or thinks they are. Take as an example, the fare I drove to the junction this evening. A good baker as ever there was. Such cakes and tarts at a sale of work last month as you'd never believe. The name on the stall was Miss Fields and very young and smiling she was as she wrapped the things up and thanked you. Behind the buns, becoming more visible as the time passed, was the person who made them. You'd have said she was settled for life.

You'd never believe the things the poor woman said about herself, as I drove her to catch the last night train passing south and stopping at the junction, it appears the dough didn't rise - so the yeast must be at fault, and if so, men were to blame.

But there she was pouring forth to the maid in the kitchen and saying how men took girls away from where they'd be well looked after, when in comes the new mistress and wants an explanation. There is one thing said and another thing being denied. There's a little bit of someone's mind here and another there, and if you were to ask someone else's opinion there would be a completely different story anyways. She'd have to work out her notice. And she'd never been given notice before, and she'd want to pack that very moment. Well, she'd have to find her own conveyance, and it was then that I was given a call.

Just proof of the opening there is for a taxi service to the country. Here we are passing the place – if you ever need a quick get away," he laughed, "telephone 123. We'll be at the Trough Inn in a few moments now. Though the bar has closed, I don't think the good lady will have put the chain on the door yet. I'll stay with you till I see you inside."

"Thank you, thank you very much, sir. There should be rights be a deduction for you keeping me company. But I can't allow pleasure to interfere with the full profits of business. I'm a Lancashire man."

"The service is well worth the fare," I said with the most genial tone I could muster.

I was glad I had had a long doze in the train so that I was wide awake, and unusually receptive during the soliloquy – certain undertones had not escaped me, and if the pleasure of the prelude was a foretaste of what I could expect from the performance, I would be content to have stepped off the train.

A light was shining through the imperfectly drawn curtains of the window at which the car drew up. "I won't stay if you don't mind." My driver murmured. "I would rather she thought it was the reputation of the house that had brought you."

"I understand," I said.

"You mayn't be so dull as you seemed half an hour ago –." He rejoined as he moved away, leaving me in front of an opening door.

"Do come in," invited a small woman, standing aside to let me pass, "there is a fire still alight in the sitting room and I can bring some cocoa in a few moments. Leave your case in the passage. I always have one bed airing with a hot water bottle so you can feel you are expected, even though it is rather late," she said this without the attitude of resentment that so often marks the speech of business owners forced into servitude. I nodded in thanks.

"That's very good-natured of you. I'll bring in my case if I may, as I want to write down a few notes while you are so kindly occupied." I passed into the lighted front room dedicated by two signs on the door to – sitting – and – writing.

"Do," I added as I stood in the opening, closing it after her, "bring in a cup for yourself and share the fire with me." And I hurriedly wrote the notes of the conversation to which I had so quietly listened.

With the cocoa ten minutes later, which I rose from my chair to welcome, came a plate of tongue sandwiches – and the extra cup.

"It isn't often that one is invited to sit down in one's own room," the low voice of a fair haired woman volunteered, as the fire settled down into the gloom of an added piece of coal, "perhaps you are an American – if I may ask – and I will know in the morning," she added smiling – "when you sign the book."

"Yes – that must stick out like bristles, but I am also a member of a secret society which is not confined to one country and its real secret isn't given away if I tell you what its motto is – you be nice to me and I'll be nice to you."

"That does make things rather cozy," she said. "Do you write like you talk?" She added in enquire, pointing to my papers.

"No, these are only to make mistakes more difficult. I earn my living by telling boys and girls to take note. If one doesn't there's always terrible confusion. I have just left a friend who never does, so if he were here in my place, and were to write to me of what you said when I first came in – you'd be bringing me shaving water in a few minutes and had hot water bottles in the bed."

"I agree that would make for confusion," she laughingly agreed. "When would you like breakfast?" she said as rose to leave.

"I hope it wasn't the shaving water that reminded you of tomorrow. Eight o'clock tomorrow, if I may."

"I'll put a lighted candle on the floor outside the door of your room. Will you see the fire looks safe, and turn out the lamp? Thank you. Good-night." And that was all of that conversation that managed to arrive on paper.

A seven-thirty scuffle outside and a rap on the door enabled me to arrive as a hairless ensemble in the sitting room at eight. On the table was a rack of toast as a consumable object, and a woolen covered teapot, but following me, and again following her, was a small child of seven carrying a plate of shredded wheat above her head.

Emily was more likely to be engaged in thought then in speech. She was a disciple of the cinema and was filled with fanciful nonsense. Monday afternoon matinees were the most affordable, convenient, considering the financial state of her family. The films, as a consequence of their accessibility, were mainly relics of a bygone era. They were black and whites from the Depression, and their optimism was not tempered by the affluence enjoyed today. It was in these cinemas that she saw the film stars, with their dewy eyes and ethereal haloes of hair. They spoke soft words, never raising their voices. In some there were princesses, and in her mind she could put herself in their place. Oftentimes, they were from deep Europe, a place she had yet to penetrate. Emily had lived in the town of Lampton for most of her young life. She knew its cobbled streets very well and all those who as of yet, played at being a part of society. On long summer days they raided the bookstore, threw stones in the river and if they had some left-over pocket change from ice cream, attended the cinema. This week's matinee featured the orient, in all of its exotic wonder. In it, there were princes were served trays of grapes on velvet pillows.

"Good morning sir," said another child of fifteen. "Its Emily. She's been to the pictures, and seen how princes are waited on. You don't mind her helping Mother and me?"

"I think it very kind of both of you to help her. Well Emily did you bring the teapot that way?"

But Emily, having put down in my place the plate, walked round the table, which was at the height of her chin, in silence and left the room.

"Ah, I see what it is, her salary would have to be doubled if she was given a speaking part. Give her my princely thank, Miss Cotton."

"Nobody has ever called me that before, sir. I'm Amy."

"Well, Amy, see there's a large tray under the bacon. I smell cooking." And Amy, who could be guessed to a certainty as the landlady's daughter, hurriedly left the room giggling.

In due course, though not through the courtesy of Emily, eggs and bacon, butter and marmalade and more toast arrived. Emily reserved herself for a bowl of water, and with beseeching eyes she urged me to wash my hands when I was finished eating.

"Tell your mother that I'll be staying another night," I said to the elder girl who was in attendance.

"She thought you might not know we have a garden – may I show it to you," and through a couple of bends in passages I was brought to a patch of grass slightly bigger than a tennis court, with a weeping willow of great age in the middle.

"But this is lovely," I said, "I'll be able to sit here and try and remember why I have come to Lambton – I think it was to take a little holiday."

"You have the right to fish you know."

"Then I can think about that here also."

The chairs don't look very comfortable," said the frank junior partner. "I mean for anyone over six feet," business acumen prompted her to add.

"No I'd have to do most of my thinking in my sleep. I'll see if there's what is called a deck chair in any of the shops. They'd be open by now I suppose. You can post it after me, when I leave."

And laughter showed me I had not a matter-of-fact Englishwoman to deal with.

"Some more tongue sandwiches will be quite enough, if I get back about one; will you tell your mother; and tell Emily I'll be back in time to put her to bed anyhow."

"Oh she wouldn't like that. She's grown up you know,"

"I'll have to find some way of reducing her age – without making her cry." I had to add as I saw a horrified look appearing in Amy's face.

A creek bound the garden, and however swift, I realized that any fishing would lie beyond the town, up or down stream. I became increasingly suspicious that the ease that seemed to be settling upon me would lead to a more prolonged stay. I immediately moved the day of departure beyond the twenty-four hours that I had mentioned to Amy. It was probably the effect of tea that would lie like a weight on my arterial system. My historic sense rejected this hypothesis when I recollected for how short a time that infusion had been operating either upon me or the people among whom I was now purposing to settle for a longer time than the usual tourist.

It was more likely contentment than tea or a tourniquet that kept one's blood from bounding one forward, a contentment half induced by the morning air that did not jump ahead of the clock. By noon or afternoon the day might be getting a little flat or the oxygen in it used up, but English morning moved slower and lasted longer than elsewhere. I was afraid I would find my writing room not yet advanced into the new day, but I was on the point of returning to it when I was presented with the Book, which was almost the sole survivor of the chained libraries of the middle Ages.

"Amy tells me you are not leaving today but would you sign the Visitor's Book?" Mrs. Cotton spoke to me.

"Certainly, but may I take it into the sitting-room so that it may eventually come out of the writing-room? I believe I left my pen there. How kind it was of you last night, Mrs. Cotton, to give me that nice fire by which to sit."

"Now where is the column where I am expected to print in large letters U.S.A? Ah here it is and I'll postpone the enjoyable half hour which I look forward to, when I will see the names of all the Majorebanks and Featherolonhaughs who have come stay here. Would you be surprised, Mrs. Cotton, if I produced a book in which I expected all hotel proprietors to sign for me?"

"I would be," she laughed but added "I am not however the proprietor. I run it for Major Fields. Oh!" and her voice ended almost in a sigh, "I spoke as if he were still alive. There was a terrible tragedy not a fortnight ago and I am not the only one who has lost a true friend. And poor Mr. Delve, too. I don't believe he came often but my bar-room is very small and fills up very soon. I pay a man who was with my husband to attend to that. He will be coming in soon to brush out and tidy up after last night. My husband was a Sergeant Major. He had served with Major Fields in the Great War. Of course Major Fields was then only a young lieutenant and my husband only a private, but they had got to know each other well in the trenches, and when the Germans broke through in March something of value my husband saved from a dug-out made him very grateful.

"They both stayed on as regulars and served in India, but Major Fields retired when his father died while my husband was in for his twenty-one years. Major Fields then let him have a farm and he married me, but went back when the New War came and died at Cologne before they crossed the

Rhine. It was then that Major Fields was so very kind, for of course I couldn't keep the farm, and he put me in here as his manager."

"And then in a moment he was gone. We mustn't think it was the river that took him – it was the mud round his boots, the water might have seemed like a relief. I don't know what I'm saying sir. I must go away. Forgive me. Amy will get anything you need."

By the time I had got into the street, the sun combined with the time of year, had raised the temperature to pleasant warmth. Sunblinds were down on the side of streets that were not so narrow as to make them unnecessary. Strolling was strenuous. A range of tinned goods here, of woolen there, of wicker beyond, I slunk past the books like a dog past the butchers. A shop with a long frontage and several entrances seemed to betoken a large lofty interior. From one of the counters percolating into the outside air came the aroma of coffee.

It was mid-morning, and the shop I entered was obviously a first class establishment – from the height of my eyes I could see fruit and vegetables – cold meats – china and glass – groceries at various centuries of small groups. I myself edged up closer to the coffee-roasting machine. A 'Miss' was being served, a girl with lovely dark unplucked eyebrows and a thin boned nose as betokened a local aristocrat. The order was being taken down and would be packaged and put aside for the customers' later call. The voice was in the clear timbre upon which a century of Englishwomen have made their reputation. The stage, broadcasting and film have now made it a matter of antiquarian wonder.

Upon, Miss, which I then knew to be a Miss Darcy, leaving the counter and darting through the door, it was found that Miss Darcy had left behind a bunch of lilies, for I saw them left on a chair and held them up for them to be identified as hers.

"Perhaps Miss Darcy had intended putting them in her car," I found myself suggesting, "Would it not be best for me to overtake her?" I had not yet released the bunch and the stare I was given neither wilted the flowers, nor me but only burnt a hole in my back as I turned and dashed away with Lancashire speed.

My speed was such that I almost ran into the girl as, only a few steps from the shop, she turned, her flowers remembered. She looked at them with a smile, rather than at me as I handed them to her.

"Miss Darcy, I must claim acquaintanceship for a few moments, after which if you think I cannot be of the least service to you, please stare me into the ground. It is not only," I started to stammer as my mind sought in vain for an appeal that would appeal, but was "-that I have always preferred Miss Darcy to Miss Bennet." A delightful laugh and eyes that had reached my face at last mercifully interrupted me.

"Not two days ago I heard almost the same words. Is this opinion being mass-produced in your country – admiration off the assembly line? You embarrass me more than reassure me, which," with a lift of her eye-brows, "I suppose this is your object?"

"It is indeed. If I could only keep my admiration, that is a more correct word than preference, and completely concealed I might succeed. If I had known who you were before I started to look at you, your appearance would have had less interest. But never thinking to ever meet you I allowed myself to be charmed while under the influence of roasting coffee beans," I continued, pointing back to the shop where we had stood side by side, "And then I heard your name mentioned. And if I could only remember what it is that I have to say, before you thank me and turn away."

"I wouldn't like to be too hard. I think you must be quite an interesting person to those who can understand what you are saying."

"Might I walk in your direction until my poise is recovered? No disgrace will attach to you; I'm neither known nor wanted by the police, and I only came to Lambton last night. Ah, I've remembered. Thank you for not thanking me."

"Could you wait?" Miss Darcy interrupted, "my mind is very full at the moment. And you see I trust you, that what you have to say is important for me to know. I set out this morning on a mission, let us reach my car, it is parked not far from here, and when I have taken these lilies to his grave, I will try and believe that mission is over,"

"You are more than good," I said, "and hope that our talk and walk though conventionally alarming will deaden your pain. I would be a poor consoler if I asked anything to subtract from what is in your heart. Is this your car? I admit defeat with any door handle. May I hold the flowers? And when I have handed them back, wait for you here?"

"I think you do really know me," she said in a tone of hesitant enquiry.

When she had gone, I was left with the memory of a face as white as the lilies and a hand as black as a prayer book. She had given me the hand in exchange for the flowers, not something you could grasp still less shake, but support for a moment: the leather taut and only just adequate for its purpose.

There is a literature of gloves, but I was not remembering it and I was also forgetting the joyful occasions when young girls carry lilies in procession. She seemed as stricken as Mrs. Cotton. And then I realized that I was only keeping my mind's eye on the glove so as not to be looking too intently into the face.

There is also a literature of faces, a literature illustrated by art, that representational art which our own generation has decided to condemn, deride and supercede. The next generation may have a deeper suggestion of anchors and triangles and buttonholes, to give deceiving names to absorbing entities, when art schools have mastered their innocence.

And I suppose I was remembering the literature as well as the art. I was one of the old grey heads, but not a yet a grey beard, looking, across the distance with Aegean sunlight on a face.

"Do talk," she spoke with a sob in her voice, when she returned twenty minutes later. "I don't want to forget myself. I want to be good and kind and cheerful. But I don't want to feel sorry for myself. I don't want to despise myself for feeling sorry for myself. Interest me in something else."

"Will you let me retrace every step from the moment I first saw you back to the moment when I had last thought of you? You may be surprised to learn of all the wonderful things that are happening in the ancient borough of Lambton. But shall we go back and discover whether that coffee tastes as good as it smells?"

"I was going there. It won't be too hot if we get a seat in the window; you perhaps noticed it is on the shady side of the street."

"On our way, could we find a toy shop? I want to buy a doll. Let me tell you the tale of the little girl who has already grown up."

Miss Darcy agreed that the doll wouldn't be allowed to grow up, and keeping a family of one from growing up would help to keep any little girl from growing up. She laughed in suggesting that they never laughed and so got old so quick.

I could be very definite on the point that if Emily's doll went to the dentist it would lose its teeth.

"Should we look at soft dolls whose teeth could be sewn on?" I said, and she, preoccupied, said,

"I'd forgotten fair-haired dolls, they were always the most loving and obedient. Everyone loved fair-haired dolls. Didn't they?"

"Yes."

"Now that sounded as if you were speaking the truth.

Did the doll have long hair?"

"She could sit on it when I first saw it brushed."

"How lovely that must have looked. Do you now of any other dolls?"

"Three."

"Any sailor boys?"

"I'd rather call them lead soldiers."

"And have any of them grown up?"

"None."

"Well there you are," and Miss Darcy's fair-haired choice was packed up by the cashier and paid for by me, while Miss Darcy said, "I never knew it was so easy to get my own way."

"Well, if time means nothing to you," I genially answered. "We must have taken a quarter of an hour."

"I'm not one to squander my time."

"No, you're being good and kind and cheerful, and that is remembering."

"How nice of you. What are you? A clergyman? I suppose I ought to know."

"Will you promise that it won't make any difference to your teaching me what I ought to think and do? – like you did about black-haired dolls."

"No, I like teaching."

"Well, I ought to be teaching you – I'm a professor."

"Oh! I'll never be able to open my mouth again,"

"But your promise?"

"It will be difficult to keep."

"We can forget your promise in the cup of coffee we have nearly reached."

The combination of smiles for Miss Darcy and scowls for me as we passed by the counter gave a hint at the spectrum of human character

"Now do tell me what it was that you wanted to say," said Miss Darcy as she relaxed a little in her seat, waiting for the coffee I had ordered.

I understood that in the backward march of time there is such a long way from Emily to what I wanted to say.

"If I tell you before one o'clock will it be all right?"

"You just want to talk? It makes no difference if I am here or not?"

"But it does; it makes all the difference. You've also to take into account the larger significance. You can hardly imagine how frustrated an American must feel when by crossing the Atlantic, he finds that instead of there being one hundred and sixty million people with whom he might talk, he only has those who will speak with him forth-right. It's like crying in the desert."

"Or worshipping a statue," she flashed with that ripple of laughter and intonation of half-enquiry which I had noted before.

"Now, you went to be good school I can see," was my following reflection. "Who taught you that?"

"First the last, and next the first. It's a little of a pretense to consider me in a Spanish master's study."

"There speaks Gloriana."

"You know the other American – the one I saw for a moment, the day before yesterday – called me Georgiana."

"Were there present, in the room below a staff of assistants who would have sprung to your assistance, Georgiana."

"I'm not swooning with the shock, am I? It would serve you right if I gave you my hand across the table, and asked you to hold it," she laughed. "But here are the coffee pots coming to separate us."

During their emptying, I told about Amy and her Mother and their background.

"There are four bedrooms, and a man comes in to run the bar. Mrs. Cotton sat talking to me last night. No, don't look at me and laugh like that. You should know this is quite a different case of vulnerability.

"I'm sorry," she said. "I won't make fun of you, if you

won't make fun of me. After all she didn't tell you her Christian name, did she?"

"No, but what you have just said about fun reminds me of what I told her was the motto of a secret society I belonged to – and I think you must be a member also. 'You be nice to me, and I'll be nice to you.'"

She hasn't the least idea, I imagine, that she appears as a daydream in the strenuous life of the garage proprietor who dropped me at her door. It is he who helps me to help you, as I believe you will think when I tell you what he said.

His reminiscences – I am indebted to an exceptional power of perception at this moment for my hint in that direction – included an account of an earlier fare – dare he also call it.

There cannot be any other place to which details can apply. Georgina's home was never mentioned, but stands in my imagination as definitely threatened.

"Oh!" there was such a sweet expelling of breath in a sign of relief from the girl that I did not continue.

"Oh, I can explain to you what people probably don't know yet. Our residence and my father were certainly in great danger till the beginning of the week. And that is probably what you heard being discussed. But then everything changed, and we are the happiest of people. Don't I seem to be enjoying myself?" with a smile.

"It must be nearly two hours since I started to try and reassure you, and I don't want to stop you smiling," I answered, "but another danger can follow on who is overcome."

"This is it. A baker had a disagreement with her new mistress. The mistress had heard remarks that seemed to show that someone she supposed to be far away had been taken further away and would never be found again. Denial and explanation made it clearer, and remorse at what she had divulged or helped to be guessed at, was what was tormenting the baker as she rode to the station, talking to the driver. Miss

Darcy could never forgive her.

The mistress wouldn't do anything immediately; she wouldn't even telephone to see if that someone, a young girl, was not really still there. Her husband was away and she would wait for his return. Her husband was the guardian of the girl and could make it difficult for the people who could not produce her. There was talk of criminal charges and humiliation.

"Can I be of the least service to you?" I ended.

I had not added to her pain or my own pity by resting my eyes on her face as I had been speaking.

When I looked up from the table surface I saw her looking across the room, over my shoulder, her mouth beautifully relaxed and yet firm.

"Ne vous derangez pas," she said in a low voice, and a moment later I felt that someone was standing behind my back.

"Good afternoon Miss Darcy, it is a long time since you were seen in Lambton," I heard a voice above me say.

"Yes, Mr. Bidwell, I have been visiting the Pleydell Bouveries on Exmoor, I would like you to meet Mr. Hope, my Father's new manager."

I had very little to guide me except a wish to please. Most fortunately I had pretended to listen to the greeting that had taken place. My cue was to remain floating and let the wave come over me. It would probably carry me towards the shore, as is the way of waves. Thus, I intended to remain sitting, a limp could later excuse me if this proved to be a rudeness.

Mr. Bidwell, for all his youth and ease, obviously felt at a disadvantage. One of the great assets secured in passing one's fortieth birthday is the aura of experience that youth cannot penetrate. Mr. Bidwell might have a very clear idea of his own generation and even of those a few years ahead, but these balding, fish-eyed seniors might be anything under heaven. Everyone was a category in himself. I could see him breaking his head against the hard wall of uncertainty. And no suggestion could be disqualified. Even if he was right, how nearer was he to knowing anything about my weaknesses or my powers?

His opening remark plainly indicated though probably not intended to do so, that Miss Darcy's appearance in Lambton had been noted and reported to him, whereupon he had set out to find her. But any easy plans he may have formed as he came to the café were now worth a good deal less.

But I didn't sit there smirking. I was the dull weight in a sack, waiting for the thrust of the bayonet. But I was capable of movement, and could add to his confusion by swinging left or right. I would be ashamed to put on paper a specimen of what I said as Mr. Darcy's manager. It wasn't ridiculous, or faulty at a single seam – probably a mystifying mixture of Company Report, Council's opinion, White Paper, and directive to a local tax collector.

Georgiana looked at me with wide-eyed interest and Mr. Bidwell said he could be hoping to see her again shortly now she had returned.

"I think you're the cleverest woman in Europe." I told Georgiana, when he had smilingly left us.

"You must be quite the cleverest actor," she laughingly replied. "I felt like a leading lady trying to give support. How fortunate that you had at last got to the point and showed me how much I needed help before he came across the room."

"What is he? I won't add like you did – A clergyman?"

"You know I rather like you to make fun of me – just a little –" she answered. "Otherwise I'd be devoured by pride. 'The cleverest woman in Europe' was it?"

"Yes, but what don't I think of Europe?"

"I don't mind – you're not talking to one of your hundred and sixty million."

"Don't rub it in what I'm missing. But was he dangerous, and do you think we have much time?"

"I can't think. I only knew when you stopped speaking and I saw Mr. Bidwell coming towards me, that I'd need your help and that your being Daddy's Manager would keep you near me. What do you mean by 'have much time'?"

"When can we expect you to get a telephone or personal call? You recognize the situation was affecting you?"

"Oh yes. It's Daddy and I who will be made to suffer, if you think they can prove wrong was done. It's a Mr. Fields. I don't know him, he left Lambton so long ago, and I don't think Daddy does. We're quite faced with the unknown – as much as you are," she added.

"Well. It was nice we had this window all to ourselves to have this talk. Could we rely on it happening again? When can I meet you? You will need a long, long rest. Tomorrow is Saturday the 20th?"

"I'll have to tell you all the facts as soon as possible, but I should get home now. I'm not the cleverest woman in Europe and I can't pretend."

"Send a message to the Trout Inn."

"Will you help to carry my groceries to the car? It'll be better than coming back tooting, and no one will stop to talk to me if you are walking with me. Here's your doll. You won't think me rude for not asking you over for lunch? You saw I was all right in an emergency, but I haven't nerves of steel and I want to be a help to you if you are helping me," she added smilingly.

"There's hope for Hope." I encouraged her to believe. My recipe would be a bath."

"I'll see you as soon as I can – and tell you all about it. It's wonderful you've arrived just in time with the warning."

One has had to be selective of remarks that fall con-tinuously like the Vallumbrosa leaves that strew the books of every earnest author. The girl is five feet four, twenty-three, sound in jaw and so on, but all human feeling is to be kept out of the falling leaves. I only knew that goodness and kindness and cheerfulness gave them their colour and value, though they were nothing but words.

I had to wait for the reopening of shops after lunch before I had time to get my easy chair, but I had spent the time of lunch itself in consuming a once living replica of the trout that swung from a pole outside. There were the tongue sandwiches also. Emily played no part in the matinée performance. I understood from Amy she was doing homework, pot-hooks having survived in this remote part of the country. When I returned with the chair and put it in the seclusion of the weeping willow I slept to good effect for an hour, wakening with the outline of an imaginative plan.

But I determined to go to 123 and find out what my driver thought of Mr. Bidwell. If I was classified in his mind as slow, how did Bidwell rate? No good to underestimate the players or the reserves. Miss Darcy had not answered, though probably inadvertently as it is termed, my question as to whom he was and was he dangerous. Perhaps all young girls consider young men who smile dangerous.

At 123 I found the driver changing the engine of a Ford. I concluded he had to be on wheels or in motion to be a complete man. He needed little more than an extra spanner in his own works. With his back on the ground and a roof over his head the protective elements of his nature went under the bench with the oiled rags.

Bidwell? He was sorry he couldn't spare the time for talk now. When I wanted him to drive me back to the junction he'd be very pleased to tell me. He knew a lot about him. There had been mention of him some time ago in *The Manchester Guardian.* He would always drop his repair work as the car was needed. He had said that if I wanted him, would I use the phone. I considered it was easier for him to hang up than for him to have to ask me to let him get on with his job.

'Mechanical moods', I thought to myself as I returned to the Inn. Here a surprise almost as great as the sudden appearance in a Lambton Coffee Room of Mr. Bidwell– lying in the deck chair, which had been removed from the shadowy obscurity of the willow, was a muslin figure. I suppose that the figure was that of Georgiana more than that it was dressed in muslin, though the material has a tendency to weave through the mind of a masculine writer. It was white, and such as had first caught my eye when she entered the sunlight, thus enhancing interest.

"I'm not going to open my eyes in case I should see that you disapprove of my coming. I suddenly felt so rested and enthusiastic after a short time alone and I determined to come and throw myself on your – deck chair. You had told me that you were the only visitor so I wouldn't run into anyone else who would be critical of my appearance – I mean my appearing. I'd like to open my eyes to see whether I have captured your attention," she added turning on one side and burying the left side of her face in a pillow.

"I've never allowed you to say three sentences together before," I answered. "This is delightful."

"I'm calling on Mrs. Cotton of course, and only staying on to see how you intend to put Emily to bed. I like Mrs. Cotton very much. While the children were bringing your throne, as they call it, into the sunlight, we had a lovely gossip together, in your writing room. We hardly mentioned you of course – women never gossip about men, they wouldn't teach other to think that men ever entered their minds."

"Well, whom were you gossiping about?"

"Mrs. Hope, may I call her?"

"You can call her, Mrs. Hope, but you shouldn't gossip about her – you don't know her."

"But women don't gossip about people they know. That would be rude in England it's the Queen's hats and shoes and things like that."

"Are you sure it wasn't my wife's hats and shoes?"

"We may have wondered what size she wore, but it was principally about how she must have spoiled you without spoiling you, if you understand what I mean?"

"So you were talking about me?"

"No, it was just general – you would be an American man, and she an American woman."

"But Mr. Hope isn't an American – I'm sure he has a British passport."

"We must have been talking about a different person then," she answered. "So you needn't worry."

"Who am I then," I weakly asked, "we ought to be agreed about that."

"Mrs. Cotton and I both agreed that you were quite the nicest man, of course, of your age who we had met."

"That leaves Mr. Bidwell still unaccounted for – I'm not jealous – I'm too conceited, but is he dangerous as an enemy or as a friend?"

"I felt that he was very dangerous as he came to interrupt our conversation. I may have been overstrung or it may be a premonition. There's a very simple explanation for his appearance' that he had learned of our sudden affluence and seemed to want to have changed sides before it became generally known, not necessarily for my benefit, but to put himself right with somebody else – someone I know – or even someone I don't."

"You certainly see the ripples reaching across the lake."

"How, lovely, can I open my eyes?" she cried. "But there's no elegant way of getting out of this chair set at this angle. Will you shut yours while I roll out?"

"You didn't see me on my hands and knees," she added as she came to my side. "So I can, if I want, imagine you think me the most beautiful woman in Europe."

"It is sometimes dangerous to speak the truth, so you will never hear me say it."

"I'd rather be told it that way than in any other," she laughed.

"Will you come in and sit by the unlighted fire where I wasn't being discussed and tell me about what happened?" I asked. "I would rather have paper by me while you are talking so that I can take notes. But first I supposed I ought to see what has happened to Emily."

"Emily was in her mother's side of the house, sitting at the table eating bread and jam. As I entered the room on hands and knees, I got rather mixed up with the chair and table legs but if Emily wouldn't speak she couldn't help laughing."

"I got the idea from Miss Darcy, she looked so funny," I explained.

"Oh you must speak the truth to children. Emily will believe every word you say, and you know you never looked," cried Georgiana.

"Yes, Miss Darcy is right," I hastened to restore my posture. "I did what I was told, and this is only make-believe like Emily's. Instead of putting you to bed Emily, I brought you this doll for you to take care of." Emily had memory of a father but she had been born with a knowledge how men could be kissed – jam and all.

"You don't mind sitting here?" I asked when that scene had ended. "Give me all the information that Mr. Fields will have, so that I can meet him on equal terms."

"Oh, you'll know much more than he ever could, when I've finished. I'm not sure if it will ease any danger, but it will be an enjoyment for me to tell you all about the girl I dearly love."

Part Two

Francesca is quite the sweetest girl you would ever have seen if I could take you back home and introduce you. It is just about six years ago that Major Fields brought her to Southermead and we have been very much together ever since. I must try not to tell you too much about you or myself will have a low idea of my character but it will be difficult to separate one from the other, if I were to go into any detail. But perhaps I will be able to interest you in telling you what I know of Francesca's life before she came. You will however agree that it is important to know the attitude of the speaker, friend or not, young or old, dark or fair, so that you can make the proper allowances.

We had a little tussle this morning about the last, and I am rather sorry now that you let me pull you over so easily, because a tiny part of Francesca's charm must have been that she was so very dark. You can't imagine what her hair was like just by looking at mine. I mean of course when she left. When she came she was a small child of twelve with her hair only a little below her shoulders. And I believe she had lost her hairbrush some months before, for it was in rather a dreadful state. I do hope I wasn't critical, for I was eighteen then and may have been inclined at first, but the interest in helping her was so immediate that I don't think I had time. I was just back from boarding-school where I had been all through the war, except of course in holidays, and though I was rather tempted to ask Daddy to go on to Oxford, for I had done well in the Higher Certificate; it made such a difference having someone to look after, and someone who looked up to me you may well be thinking, and my 'schoolgirl ambitions', I think they are called, soon faded.

You will be wondering about the hairbrush. Well, having explained that I'm a friend, six years older, and not quite as dark, I'll go on to that by telling you that Francesca was a displaced person. She had been found, put in a truck, and taken to a children's home. This was in the North of Italy just before the Germans laid down their arms. You see Francesca is Italian. When she came here she couldn't speak any English' that was the first thing I had to do, to tutor her. She was a very silent little thing also which made it a little more difficult but after a time delightful, she had such a lovely voice that one found a new pleasure in one's own language. But it was only after months and months of slow speech that she began to speak as quickly as I do.

I think she had been terribly shocked by that ride in the truck. It was not the last shock; being put in the home and kept there with more than a hundred other children was much more terrifying but the movement and the noise and not knowing where she was going and wanting to stay where her mummy would find her made her horribly ill. She hadn't quite given up believing that she'd see her mother again. They had always been together before that day when her Mother had gone back to Brescia.

Francesca had gone down to the little harbor, through the gate of the medieval wall, to say a short good-bye to her mother. The steamer was on its northbound passage so she had then had to run with the servant, her old nurse, to the west of the peninsula to see it out of sight. Far to the south, beyond the plain and the river and the plain and the hills, there was fighting going on between two sets of invaders of Italy, - I don't know how anyone can forgive these things.

That night Brescia, in all its inoffensiveness, was bombed and amongst the rubble of the eighteenth century home, Francesca's mother died. Francesca did not know this, and I suppose, as the Casa was closed, it would not have been generally known that the mistress was lying in the ruins. I would like to tell you the story of Francesca's mother, as I remember Major Fields telling it to me.

Major Fields knew part of it – he left me as an adult to imagine other parts of it he said – O dear; may I borrow your hanky for a minute. That was very silly of me. Francesca's story is sad enough, for she was waiting for her mummy to come back. Her old nurse told her that mummy had gone to look after the wounded, but that didn't make it any easier for a little girl, whatever older people might think. The nurse was fine, even though her heart separated her from the truth, and of course there was the first uncertainty. There was nothing left in Brescia – home, furniture, tapestries, papers; everything had disappeared, as though God had forgotten. There was only the villa at Sirmione and a little money in one of the drawers, besides quite simple furnishings. But the nurse took charge and saw that Francesca still kept on with her violin practice, and sold such things as she could get value for, so that there would be money for the next few years.

Then months later came the troops, the villa was requisitioned and enquiry was made about the sad little girl. The nurse had told one lie about the mother and, much as she would have loved to say that Francesca was her own, she said she was an orphan without any relatives that she knew. Because the old Brescian family had actually died out except for Francesca without any co-lateral branches. And the truth was much more fatal than the falsehood, for it proved that she had no right over the little girl who would be taken away to live with the other war orphans. It was an awful scene in Francesca's mind.

She was taken off, with nothing of her own, and that was when she stopped brushing her hair except for a few moments, when one really needs ten minutes a day; and became silent. She was almost stupid and most terribly thin when her uncle found her.

Are you surprised to find she had an uncle, and have you guessed it was Major Fields? Her father had been Major Fields' younger brother, but that is the story I am not to tell you. Major Fields was serving in Italy and as soon as Brescia was in allied hands he dashed over from the Adriatic. Of course a Communist mayor had been put in charge – for that was the American policy – a ration card and party membership issued by the same hand at the same time. And an enquiry about a Princess, Francesca's mother was not given any attention. The family lawyer had also suffered destruction at the time of the bombing, which may have explained why the Nurse had been left alone.

And then there happened what would happen in Italy. I have never been to Italy; this is what Major Fields said. Some perfectly impossible looking individual presented himself in a quiet street with all the information, a Mr. Vanier. Date and details of the bombing, knowledge of the mistress's return the day before' without the Signorina who had not returned at any later date, so would still be at Sirmione. On many occasions la Principessa had smiled to him, she had inwardly recognized that he would have always done her the most desperate service. No, it had never occurred to him to enter into her employment. It might be enough that he had now been able to render some slight service, when otherwise, without this he hoped forgiven interference. He might, it was true, eventually regret his behavior, he had often in life had occasion to do so, but never this his action which as prompted by his recognition of what la Principessa would have expected of him – he unworthily surmised, did expect of him.

I believe he spoke like this to Major Fields, not only because he loved the Principessa, but he as drawn out of himself by the nobility of the Englishman. He was not to know that he was speaking to the brother of the Principessa's husband. That again may have attracted him.

In Sirmione Francesca had not been found. The unit, which was dug in at the villa, was incredulous that anybody of any concern to a brass-hat had ever been in their line of vision. If the old nurse, who failed to qualify for belief owing to a squint, had said her charge was well-born, that went without saying. Everyone in Italy with a roof over their heads seemed to think they were princes. Major Fields was made perfectly frantic by the competent ignorance and dislike of everyone whom he questioned.

You will never be able to realize; not having known him how quietly and steadily he will have outstayed every welcome as he persisted in enquiry. He waited for something more to materialize, that he might trace that of the track of a bare foot as it left. The people with whom he was in touch were profoundly unconcerned, though a missal and veil, which must have had an owner, were handed him, but he felt that eventually, he would meet someone whose business it had been to conceal the child. There had been, he found, through other native sources, someone... and then there had been no one.

The answer came on his desk shortly after he had returned to duty. Details of requirements –trucks – personnel and supplies for an organization handling uprooted children. They seemed to be somewhere in his neighborhood, along the Brentz. It was no holiday when he started his search, but he felt he had a master - question which would make it a short one.

"Have you a child who is very different from her companions?" the question was passed down until it reached an observant attendant.

"Would you take me to her?" He followed.

"This is my niece," he had then said as he held her hand.

There was much irregularity in his taking her; objection was made, the numbers would not tally. He signed a receipt, and she cuddled up to him shivering in the cold as he was driven back.

The war was over. As a retired officer from the reserve, he was not tightly bound, and the thin, silent but happy little girl was soon in her uncle's home. He was always very concerned about his health; she started to grow rapidly with additional sleep and the change of food and with the age she had reached. Dr. Carter quite agreed that she should not go to school, or indeed be put under any mental strain.

It was found she played the violin and this she practiced without any fatigue showing, and eventually she began to talk as I have said, and I was to encourage her in both instruments. I could not have had six happier years than the last six. I was away for short periods at times, but we saw each other every-day when I was at home, for she never left Southmead.

Major Fields did not have a car – he and Francesca walked if they came into Lambton. In fact after Father gave me mine three years ago Francesca never would come into it. But our residence and Southmead are not two miles apart and I expect I was more often there. It is on the way in, even if I wasn't going there on purpose to stay for some time. And could you believe it possible, when the great tragedy came to the life of Francesca and her uncle, I was neither there nor knew anything about it. One week ago yesterday he was buried.

This change was so startling that it didn't seem as if Francesca had grieved at all that I had not come to her. She was not at the funeral so she had not known we were not there. Lord Mountsey, you must understand, not only has no telephone to but also takes in no newspaper. You'd enjoy him very much I am sure. He is building a castle and is almost as eccentric as a professor. He still rides to hounds and must be nearly eighty. And there we were, quite cut off from the world.

But in our absence besides Francesca's new friend, there also arrived Major Fields' younger brother, who has now inherited the estate. There had been three boys: Major Fields, this Mr. Fields and Francesca's father. The two last left Lambton as soon as they grew up and never returned – in the case of Mr. Fields that must have been nearly thirty years ago. He went into business and never visited his brother. He was not very pleased to find a niece in the nest when he came down for the funeral, as he had made all his arrangements to settle in, having lately sold his home. However, Francesca was to be sent to an overdue education and will eventually end up as another woman in industry.

What terrified her most was that she felt those all around her were beginning to doubt her personality. She realized by Sunday that Major Fields had never returned to Italy after the war, and therefore had no more paper proof of who she was. It was even possible that the man she might be shifted onto was capable of anticipation.

She arrived for protection on Monday evening and Daddy being in his study was able to telephone to Southmead that she would be stopping 'til her leg, which limped, was better. Next morning it seemed to have been arranged that she was going to Canada, and Daddy and I just fell in openmouthed and openminded with her plans. Everything presented itself as inevitable; but this wouldn't be a defence in law I suppose. She wasn't just a girl who had run away from home, but a girl for whom daddy had made himself answerable to.

We must have been designed by providence to keep her free and happy. I shall miss her terribly myself, but I cannot doubt that this is the best that could have happened. And wasn't your coming to Lambton, and even hearing what she had said, with my name mentioned, and then meeting me, and my listening to you, and your warning me in time for me to see you were my hope, all designed by providence?

While Georgina recounted her story I let out a gasp when she mentioned Vanier, the clerk and my acquaintance. How could I have imagined that his doings would have resulted in something so wonderful?

"I don't know what your tale would sound like if it was put on paper and then read," I spoke for the first time, "but it has sounded lovely from your voice. Firstly you need not worry, but it would not be professional if I made the solution of the problem facing us look too simple - it will surely require frequent consultation. I have been in the habit of meeting most of my university classes everyday, so that will entail no change in my routine. Before I leave, and I must do so soon, I will have to acquire your address so that I may send my recommendations by post. Most certainly I will have some ideas by Monday, my letters will be your morning lecture!"

"I do however remember," I added, "when I was a young married instructor at Cornell, the Sororities, which may need explaining to you, did believe that I am telling you the truth, and your not having gone to Oxford may make that easier, I am quite willing to have a little kindness shown me. Where I am now there are no Sororities and I don't remember ever meeting any professors at those parties, the girls were either frightened of them or thought we would be. When I do visit at some juncture in our long days, then you have two perfectly good reasons for economizing on a plate of bread and butter on Sunday afternoon when I am inclined to travel."

"I do need 'Sororities' explained," Georgiana agreed laughing, "while they blushed feminine in gender, they were singular in person,"

"Oh it's only the adaption of a happy idea to local conditions," I almost blushed in hastily explaining. "There were lots of them and they didn't pretend to be our sisters – we had our wives with us anyhow."

"The similarity would seem to be very vague," said Georgiana, resting her chin on the backs or her two hands.

"You needn't butter the bread," I suggested.

"You mean that if I didn't, all this similarity would have vanished, and you would confess you had failed to introduce an American custom?"

"Oh, an English afternoon tea is good enough for me, if you are thinking of that."

"No, I rather like the idea of instructors – I am sure they could stand a little explaining likewise. Do come," she said, clapping her hands. "I'll be awfully pleased to see you."

"There is one thing; to be a little more serious than one can be over the day after tomorrow's jam" I continued, "if you get any enquiry by telephone from Southmead, be evasive to vanishing point. I imagine that type of call will precede a personal one. Am I right in thinking that no connection at present exists between the two places?"

"Yes, I haven't called, as I should do. Of course it is not yet known whether the Fields have come to stay. I don't know how this fact is established. I suppose the delivery boys decide that question and then pass their decision up the line until it reaches the local gentry as we are called."

"How thrilled I am to be in their orbit." I confessed. "You know in republican saxondom we have nothing like it. The country is strictly reserved for farmers, except in the east where a few millionaires call to each other across wide intervals of sludge. You either have an English butler or drive up to a hot dog stand."

"But what will Francesca do? Though she did not seem to notice she was in a car on Wednesday; that was an exceptional occasion and I don't believe she would want to go anywhere except on foot."

"How curious! She may find a few million like herself but they are never mentioned. They survived to a small extent in the university world – you notice it is called a world as thought moving in a different space."

"My sudden alarm was needless, she will be living in a forest and sleeping in a cabin. The dogs will have to walk to her."

"Like I'll be walking up on Sunday. The point to return there, is that it might be better not to have committed oneself on to whether Francesca is with you or not, until I am ready to spring my great surprise and, as you are clever enough to realize, there was never a great surprised without a great deal of preparation behind it."

"So you already have a reason why I need not worry?"

"Your conversation is full of suggestions and I am almost sure that our side will win. But it will be easier if we all decide to pull at the same time. How many are there? I mean is Mr. Darcy leaning back at the end of the rope?"

"Oh you don't know, daddy," she laughed. "He is much more like Uncle Sam than John Bull. Why are all American men as round as butterballs?"

"That's a fair enough question – it should be faced – but give me my answer."

"I don't think he would be a help – if your plan can dispense with him. I couldn't say anything at lunch because I needed to see you first and then when he suggested going to Mallock for the weekend he was thinking of taking baths for his bruised leg – I didn't say anything to dissuade him."

"Are you sure you are not more his manager than I am?" I could not help innocently asking.

"Well I have been in the business nearly a quarter of a century", was her sufficient answer. "If you would give me your card," she continued," I thought he should have a manager with authority, to say that everything would be attended to, or some such formula."

"Splendid – and if he receives a telephone call or visit with the object of finding or demanding the former Miss Fields tell him to stand pat on that phrase."

"You are very encouraging." Georgiana said. "I will let you know as soon as I hear that Mr. Fields has returned, and you tell me as soon as you can, what is going to be done. I'll be going now. Were you pleased to see me? I honestly kept my eyes shut so I do not know."

"Don't speak of mine. I had just returned from a thirsty visit to the fountain when I found you lying in the chair. It would cost me the sum of drive to find out details bearing on the unfortunate birth, horrid features, dastardly career and unwelcome appearance of Mr. Bidwell."

"May I wake you from the nightmare," Georgiana enquired. "I am afraid my mind recoiled from thinking about him, surely to you satisfaction; so that I never told you who he is – the junior partner in a firm of lawyers. They are not our lawyers – you will have found that no town is so small as not to have two. As his father's is the other name on the window, he is a little more important than the first description implies."

"Do you think 'Bidwell and Bidwell' would be the Fields?"

"They are, I am sure."

"Left in rather an unused condition, can I hope?"

"You can be certain of it, if you are supposing that Major Fields never went to law in his life. His property had dwindled before he came into it – he never seemed ambitious to become more important. I believe he was changing – all sorts of wonderful changes – when he died."

"I can assure you of this," I spoke as tenderly as I could, "that in these last six years he must have grown to love you – because of Francesca, and because of yourself."

Her smile was thanks. We were not at the door.

"I left my car at the river, will you see me off a third time?" she asked. And I got into step by her side. "I'll be looking forward to Sunday." She continued, "when you may be able to divulge your plan – you know you seem to be able to keep the incident on quite a light level miles away from the police station we are just passing. Oh that is Mr. Bidwell in front of us in flannels, he must be returning from a tennis party, he is walking with Dolly Candish, they're just crossing the street to take the turning leading to the vicarage – she's the vicar's daughter. So I'm now responsible for your knowing the names of two Lambton people.

"Three; if I am permitted to contradict. I can never thank you enough for introducing me to Mr. Hope. By the by do take care of yourself till I meet you again. The greatest responsibility of running an estate I find it the health and happiness of the staff."

"Then you can have a trouble in the world. Thank-you for a most exciting day and your great kindness. When you write to your wife do send her my blessings, and I'm sure I'd love the dolls and the lead soldiers. I seem to be starting without difficulty. Good-night. I may remember some of the nice things you've said?"

And Georgiana had driven off again. Her face was still white in the approaching dusk but I could no longer compare it with lilies, the symbol of death. There would always be more happiness than its opposite in that quick mind and affectionate heart. It was where it would always be found, already within her.

As my way took me along the lake it came upon me that, if I could borrow a rod at the Inn, I would end the day by casting a fly. The evening would not be so dark but then I could follow a direction that led me to the stretch available for visitors. In silence and with the slightest bit of indolence, our affairs would soon be set in order. This must be the design set out for us.

Part Three

Upon my arrival at the lake outside of the town, I was greeted with a most extraordinary sight. It seemed like the air was comprise of the *essence* of green. The ripples of the water licked at the shoreline of the lake, like the slow trickling of time and the words that mark its passing. A silvery fish leaped out of the water and its scales were lit in rapid increments as its body plunged back into the water. A smooth wave made its way to my feet, and I shivered. The fish, which I knew would evade my rod, was large and muscles were creasing through its side. I could not know how long it has been swimming, circling the island in the middle of the lake. A swan turned its ancient head towards me, its feathery bodice looked to me like muslin. I tried to shake that image of Georgiana from my head. Slowly, the swan dipped its foot into the water, bobbing faintly in my sight from undulations derived from under my boot. The water broke in subtle and unpredictable ways. Chaos, in the way that droplets form circles that intersect one another, had a geometry to it. On the opposite shoreline I could see Mr. Bidwell lingering there with his accompaniment, Dolly Candish. Their image flickered dark against the sloshing water. They didn't see me I was sure. They seemed to be discussing something of great importance or controversy, for they were obtusely articulating and making grandiose gesticulations. I could hear their murmuring, but their words dissipated along with the English mist hovering over the surface of the water.

By this time the sun had descended to the point where its domed form was entirely visible, cutting through the trees and turning the mist into opaque walls of light. The pastoral glare was tarnished by what sounded like hooting beasts, what I knew to be the ferocious Mr. Bidwell. I could no longer think of words as coming out of a machine, but having a more organic quality to them, they were not to be digested, but felt. As the guttural speech of Mr. Bidwell presented themselves to my ears I could feel my own disgust acutely. My ears, instead of receiving a shipment of words as they usually do, parceled according to their dictionary specifications, were tainted by what seemed to me a sort of residue language leaves behind. It was bundled together in a glob of animal intonation. I then turned my focus on the pillars of light presenting themselves before me. How I could spend eternity here, suspended in a time marked at an even pace with the a succession of adjectives, each collecting a small bit of beauty in their limited but flexible capacities. I thought of what now seemed to me to be the wholeness of time. I felt the gaze of a deer deep in the woods. I felt the minnows break from their eggs; I felt them squirm onto land with their newly grown legs; I felt them lay eggs of their own. I felt the tackle at the bottom of a dilapidated boat chime and crash. I felt the sun. I felt a duck chastising one of its wayward brood. I felt a brush of wind put into motion by the distant swan. I felt a sudden fear strike me. Though my intervention in Miss Darcy's life had saved her from the clutches of Mr. Bidwell, our story could not yet be over. For if our clever words could be ripped from their gears, thrown into other times, if they did not have the finality we thought they did, they could be used against us by a devious lawyer such as Mr. Bidwell. I panicked, but soon remembered the cheerfulness intrinsic within that girl. I reflected on her earlier visit to the cemetery and her curious ability not only to recover from the pain of saying good-bye to a loved one, but also her capacity to keep them forever in her heart.

Though Mr. Bidwell was sure to pose a threat in the future, Georgiana would be certain to keep our clever defense happily in her mind, so that she will be reminded of her glory in dark times. Though I could no longer think of time as unfolding in a linear, belting manner, sometimes marked by language with an event worth recording, I could take solace in the fact that all events could be taken, for better or for worse, to affect the whole. That was what I was counting on. Georgiana, her good friend, had been taken from her by providence to a foreign country. Her good fortune will be maintained by her labours, as destiny favours those who work for their fill. In Defoe's Halifax, where the citizens carry on a manufacture which can no where be so easily supplied with the conveniences necessary to it. The manufacturing I have done with my tongue could hope to put everything in the proper patterns of motion, orbiting peacefully through the cosmos. The screeching of Mr. Bidwell across the water was ominous, like a dripping stalactite deep in a crystal-filled cave. The cacophony he created did nothing to hamper the visual enormity of the scene.

After putting away the rod and kissing the girls good night I felt it was my time to depart. There would be a courtesy train leaving late that night for London to put a handful of people back in their rightful place, and I was to be one of them.

The hissing and rumbling beast pulled away from the station and Lambton became insignificant in my line of sight. The train chugged on, with its belting power, closer to a place where my faith in fate would be tested. The imperceptible, rattling on of time was the undertone to its cyclical rhythm that I had so recently discovered. The rhythm of the train itself, though, was enough to set me to sleep. In my dreamy state I was again reminded of Defoe, but in my own way.

The train rounded a hill and the London came into view. As it drew nearer the density of houses increased until the countryside faded into memory. The rows of lodgings were crowded together so that the pattern created by their rooftops resembled a corrugated metal sheet, stretching for an immeasurable length into the horizon. These homes had no garden or pleasant stream to hold reptile or other aquatic phenomenon.

It was unclear in what industry the houses engaged themselves, but for laundry, evidenced by the lines of white undershirts. It was as though the residences were making a big show at surrender with their succession of white cloths. The whiteness streaking past the train marked the time like a ticking clock. The train slowed to accommodate the threat of obstructions that crowded cities pose.

Along the track, out of every house rose a chimney, much thinner and more sinister than the portly chimneys that are a common fixture in rural areas. They lacked any individualized infrastructure, a well or an outhouse, the self-sufficiency required of more scattered society. They were instead a part of a larger conglomerate meant to satisfy the needs of the whole.

The land, once occupied by sheep and solitary trees contained the labours of a dense population. Swathes of people enter in and out of public buildings: banks, post offices, libraries. The routes through which people pass, otherwise vacant, are now bustling with activity. The volume of which would astonish a man of the previous century.

There are little beggars or idlers, because when there are they receive little charity or compassion. They live long but only in the aimlessness of a bureaucratic job, and share a sense of entitlement which allows them the time to demand greater benefits or decline their presence at a day of work, feigning sickness or the sort. Their labour affords them their riches as well as their dispassionate souls.

I stood at the corner of a busy intersection in the middle of the city. My briefcase remained idle at my side, dissimilar to my companions, who had the habit of swinging their cases perilously to and fro, so that an explosion of paper was not uncommon. However, that collisions or eruptions were not as prevalent as I would think confounded me. Though those who passed by were within inches of each other, in the minds of these city-dwellers no one existed but themselves. I thought briefly of that man, Mr. Hope, before stepping into the crowd myself in anticipation of new students.

Sitting in my communal office, the combined brightness of the lamps and the skylights washed out my sense of sight. I again hear those voices stifled by the glow and the air of production. They are dark and guttural and somehow committed to deadlines and timetables. We professors cannot be trusted to depend on the fullness of time to complete our work. I walked down the hallway, my pace was unvaried despite wide range of people in varying states of hurry, from relaxed to frantic. My stride remained consistent as I walked through the side door of a crowded hall, the tapping of my shoes resonated in the silence that received my entrance. Now centered at the head of the room, I opened my mouth and prepared to pass on my story.

Finis.

www.ingramcontent.com/pod-product-compliance
Lightning Source LLC
Chambersburg PA
CBHW030655110726
47901CB00002B/723